To le (handwritten)

CW00779889

Red Skye Sunset

by

Hilary Orme

(author's signature)

This is the second book in the *Megan Waterfield* series.

It is the sequel to *Past the Town of Tribulation*

& Straight on to Derring Do

Cover design by Rebecca Jackson of Feathertree

Chapter 1

"What sort of name is 'Blender'?" wheezed Billy O.

"BEL-IN-DA! Her name's Belinda, not Blender," insisted Boat Boy Bob.

"All right, young 'un. I'm a bit deaf, but not the slightest bit daft!" chuckled the old man.

Billy O, Boat Boy Bob and I were sitting at the end of the pier head in the Old Harbour. We had watched as a car, driven by Bob's father, had stopped at the gate and a girl of about thirteen had got out. Mr Robertson had driven away so quickly that he had sent a shower of small stones and dust across the car park, much to the annoyance of the girl.

"The Chief Steward's got a blender," Billy O continued. "She puts in all manner of scraps, presses a button and turns out a dog's dinner!"

He nodded towards the girl and added, "That looks like a dog's dinner to me!"

In the cosy cottage Billy O shared with his sister on the edge of the town, he was Captain William O'Donnell, Master and Commander of all things, with the exception of the kitchen, that is. A sign above its door said that it was the *Galley*, the one area of their home that was under his sister's rule, and where she was known as the 'Chief Steward'.

Bob managed to raise a faint smile at the thought of his annoying cousin being a dog's dinner, but this quickly disappeared as Blender flicked the dust from her jacket and started down the path towards us. The *Dans Vers* was moored near to the pontoon where Miss Danvers, who was known to have a particular dislike of most teenagers, was unloading the contents of her luxury yacht before closing it up for the winter. We watched as Blender fixed a mobile phone to the end of a long stick, and puckering her lips into an exaggerated pout, set about taking a number of photographs of herself, while making sure that the grand yacht featured prominently in the background.

Bob held his head in his hands and muttered, "Thanks a lot, Dad! Thanks for dumping her on me."

We were too far away to hear what was said, but the appearance of Miss Danvers on deck, the exchange of a few words and a dismissive wave of her hand, resulted in Blender hastily leaving the pontoon and continuing along the path towards us.

"Cooee, Bob," she called as she got closer. "Come and take a few shots of me by that lamp thingy at the end of this stone thingy. My selfie-stick's not long enough and I want to post a few photos online so that my friends can see what I'm up to."

"Selfie-stick," muttered Billy O. "More like a *selfish* stick!"

I watched as Bob followed her along the quayside to the end of the stone pier that jutted out into the River Severn.

Billy O shook his head and gave a heavy sigh. He was very loyal to those he cared for, and as he had been my grandfather's best friend when they had served together in the Royal Navy, saw it as his duty to look after my grandmother now that she was alone. Partly out of respect, and partly because of his affection for her, he always called Grandma, 'The Captain's Wife'. As for me, I was always 'Gran'daughter' or 'young 'un'.

Each day during the sailing season, he would sit on his 'Watch', as he called it. From a battered, old deck chair at the end of the pier, he would scan the mighty River Severn from the bridges down river, up to the great horseshoe bend at Awre. There, it ran out of view and continued its journey on to Gloucester. Each day, he watched the river's rise and fall, greeted the procession of people who came to walk their dogs around the Old Harbour and noted the names of the boats that passed in and out of the great lock gates. He surveyed the drifting seaweed, the silt, the shifting sandbanks, the seagulls and the great ships as they steered their difficult course into Sharpness. He knew everything there was to know about the waters on the other side of the lock gate, but he shook his head in disbelief as he watched this strange girl adopting a number of elaborate poses near to the edge of the dock.

"Poutin', shoutin' and loutin," he observed. "I bet her friends aren't missing her one bit."

"They probably are," I mumbled, "because they're almost certainly *just* like her."

"Handsome is as handsome does," he observed.

One thing that Billy O and my grandmother had in common was their fondness for saying things in a way that most people had stopped doing years ago, and this was one of her particular favourites.

When I had first come to stay with her at *Graymalkin Cottage* for six weeks in the summer holiday, my mother had said, 'Better not ask', whenever Grandma said something unusual. However, after a few days, I had decided to find out the meanings of some of her strange sayings. I was always glad when I did so, because sometimes they were funny, sometimes clever and sometimes downright confusing, even to Grandma herself.

"I think the Captain's Wife could do with a hand," wheezed Billy O, nodding in the direction of the inner harbour where Grandma's boat, the *Fiona,* was moored. I suspected that the reason he wanted me to go over to help my grandmother was nothing to do with the fact that she needed me. I could not see her from where we were, but knew that she would be happily packing the contents of the *Fiona* into plastic boxes. She would be making everything ready to load into the Land Rover, so that it could be put into dry storage for the winter. Grandma had told me that Billy O had an illness that could not be cured, or as he put it, 'his old bones creaked and his lungs were too full of sea salt to be of any use'. I was not sure if he wanted me to go because the effort of talking to me was tiring him, or if he could see how upset I was that my friend, Bob, had been taken over by this unpleasant newcomer.

I kissed him on his whiskery, old cheeks and set off along the black, cinder path that ran up above the lock, keeping the River Severn to the left and the inner basin to the right. I dragged my feet so heavily through the loose stones that with each step, a small puff of dust was thrown high into the air. At the point where the path widened, I turned right and, finding a wooden gate in a gap in the hedgerow, lifted the rope loop that kept it closed and passed through. On the other side, a flight of stone steps led down onto a path that took me past a row of boats. Some were little more than derelict, abandoned hulks, but others, like my grandmother's, were cared for and well-kept. Towards the far end of the path I could see a large, wooden trawler, neglected for many years and known to all of the children who came to the Old Harbour as the 'Rat Boat'. On many occasions in the past, my footsteps had disturbed the boat's repulsive rodents and caused them to dive deep into the dark waters between the hull and the path. Then my pace would quicken and I would keep as far to the right of the track as the brambles would allow, hurrying on to the next berth where my grandmother's boat was moored. Today, I paid no attention to the sound of scuttling and splashing in the water beside me, because my mind was on other matters.

"Oh dear," came a voice from the *Fiona* as I climbed on board. "Someone has a face as long as a wet weekend!"

I did not need to ask my grandmother to explain this strange saying, because I knew exactly what she meant.

"Bob's friend?" she asked.

I nodded.

"She's mean and bossy and selfish and ... and ..."

"... And she's taken your friend away?" Grandma finished my sentence.

She was always very good at knowing what was *really* on my mind. I nodded sadly and sat down in the small space between a large, plastic crate and a coiled rope mat that had been fashioned from an old mooring line. On the mat lay Dotty, Grandma's Bengal cat. I stroked her gently and she responded with her characteristic half-chirp, half-bark.

"Oh well," teased my grandmother, "I'm afraid that you are stuck with your boring old Grandma."

I smiled, because if there was one thing that I had learnt about my grandmother, it was that she was *never* boring.

"It wouldn't be so bad if we could sail off somewhere and leave Blender behind," I said. I looked at the plastic boxes into which the *Fiona*'s contents were being packed, and as I gazed into the empty cabins below me, I knew that there would be no more sailing this year.

"The sailing season is over until the spring," said Grandma.

"But the sun is shining and the winds are light. It would be a perfect day to be out on the water," I said.

"There's a season for a reason!" chanted Grandma, as if she had said it many times in the past. Before I could ask her about the meaning of this latest strange saying, she had disappeared into the cabin below, emerging a few seconds later with a black, leather book in her hands. She moved the plastic crate onto the floor, so that she could sit next to me and carefully placing the book on her lap, ran her fingers over the faded, gold lettering on its worn cover. This was the log book of the *Fiona* and she was proud of this record. It gave a detailed account of every trip that she and my grandfather had made on their sailing boat and she turned the pages with care and respect. She stopped at an entry near to the beginning of the book and tapped the page, inviting me to read the words written in bold capitals at the top:

'NEVER AGAIN', they said, then underneath was added, 'There's a season for a reason!'.

"For many years, your grandfather was a captain in the Royal Navy," she began, "but although he knew everything there was to know about ships with engines, in the beginning he didn't know very much at all about sailing boats. We decided that we would learn as quickly as possible, so we bought the *Fiona* and in the first year, sailed as often as we could. Each time we went out through the lock gates and down the River Severn, our confidence grew. In fact, it grew a little bit too much, as you will see. That year, the weather was often too wet or too windy to go out, even as far as the Bristol Channel. With great sadness, we saw the sailing season coming to an end and all around us, people began to make their boats ready for the winter. Each day, we watched as more and more of them carried the contents of their boats to their cars. They would wave and call out, 'See you in the spring!' and be gone."

A small sound on the footway above us made my grandmother pause, and we both looked up at the waving branches of a large hazel tree at the top of the bank. Although there was not the slightest breeze, it swayed so violently that a flurry of leaves tumbled on to the path alongside us, like a golden snowstorm.

"Even the squirrels know how important it is to take note of the season," Grandma said. A stone fell helter skelter down the bank, followed by another shower of leaves. As I looked up, a dark figure scurried quickly out of the cover of the tree's upper branches and was lost from view, as it blended into the thick hedgerow along the edge of the track above us.

"Big squirrels," I said and could not rid myself of the idea that someone was watching us.

"Well," Grandma continued her story, "Hallowe'en arrived and it was a glorious day, so four of us decided to make the short journey down to Portishead. We planned to stay overnight in the marina and return early the next morning. The sun shone and the wind was so light that all four of us were able to drift with the tide. For once, the Bristol Channel was like a millpond, so calm that we rafted together and were able to pass food and drink between our boats. We shared our Ship's Stew and apple pies, while others offered crusty bread and lashings of ginger beer. It was as if we were cut off from the outside world: we could have been anywhere, and nowhere at the same time. One captain played his squeezebox and we all sang sea shanties at the top of our voices. Finally, the sun sank low in the sky and we made our way into Portishead in the twilight.

High water at the Old Harbour was forecast to be at ten-thirty the next morning, so as soon as we had finished breakfast, we passed out of the great lock gates at Portishead and into the Bristol Channel. Ahead of us, we could just make out the Second Severn Crossing, looking just like a lacy, spider's web. As we watched, it slowly faded from view and a thick fog rolled in before you could say, 'Jack Robinson'."

I was so gripped by the story, that I didn't consider interrupting Grandma to ask who on earth, 'Jack Robinson' was. Anyway, it would have been unlikely that she would have had the faintest idea.

"By now, it was too late to turn back as the tide would have been against us and, being a sailing boat with a small engine, the *Fiona* would not have been able to resist the fast-flowing spring tide."

Billy O had told me the difference between spring tides and neap tides. I knew that spring tides had nothing to do with the season, but that they happen when the sun and the moon line up, usually around the times of the new moon and the full moon. This means the sun and moon can work together to pull the waters of the Earth more strongly and this causes the water to rise higher. On the other hand, neap tides happen when the moon is waxing or waning and is at right angles to the sun. That means that they are pulling in different directions and the result is smaller tides.

He told me that, 'When the sun and the moon waste their energy in fighting one another, there's not much left to move the water to and fro, but when they pull in the same direction, then you'd better batten down yer bunkers!'

So that I would remember the difference between the two, I put a picture in my mind of the water 'springing' up high on a spring tide and lying in a heap on a neap.

"Before we had even reached the first bridge," Grandma continued, "the fog was so thick that you could not even see the bow of the boat. All around us, we could hear the sound of fog horns, so we knew that the others in our little fleet were safe and close by. Occasionally, one would emerge from the swirling mists, only to disappear again within seconds. We passed under the new bridge without incident, guided by the automatic fog horn that boomed above us.

With no land in sight, I was unable to check our course against any landmarks, because none could be seen. I would call out the compass bearing, watching the depth gauge like a hawk, while Granddad steered us through the dense fog, keeping to the course I had given him. It was then that we found out that the Fiona's compass was not entirely accurate. I knew that we must be near a safe passage close to the bridge, called 'The Shoots'. Sailors are guided through it by four great metal beacons.

Suddenly, Granddad cried out, "Whoa!" as he pulled hard on the tiller, causing us to lurch to starboard. I looked up to see a blur of red close to our port side. The *Lady Bench Beacon*, four times as high as a house and made from great rings of reinforced concrete, loomed out of the mist.

I think your grandfather could see that I had turned very pale, so he tried to make a joke about it.

"Missed!" he laughed nervously. "Well, at least we know where we are," he said. "Now you'll be able to check our course!"

I bent low over the chart, confused by the fact that we appeared to be far too close to the edge of the channel, despite the compass bearing showing that we should have been safely within it by now. With the chart plotter and dividers, I carefully marked and measured the course that we would need to follow to bring us safely under the next bridge and back to the Old Harbour. Minutes passed. I continued to check the compass and the depth gauge and was satisfied that we were on course, when I heard Granddad call out once more,

'A tanker!' he shouted, 'Straight ahead. It's going to hit us!' I was puzzled for a moment, as we had been listening for warnings of shipping movements on our radio and had heard none. Large ships move much more quickly than small boats and it would be unlikely that the tanker would be able to see us in the fog. Your grandfather pulled hard on the tiller, causing us to lurch to starboard once again, while I braced myself for the impact.

Thankfully, it didn't come, because that old tanker turned out to be nothing more than one of the concrete piers of the Severn Bridge, which we narrowly missed.

For two hours or more, we motored on, listening for the fog horn signals of our fellow sailors. My head and eyes ached with the effort of constantly peering into the mists in an attempt to find something that would reassure us that we were on the right track, as I no longer felt able to trust our compass.

No sooner had the words, 'We must be close to the Old Harbour,' left your grandfather's lips, when out of the mists loomed the north pier. Once again, your grandfather pulled hard on the tiller and this time, we lurched to port, missing the wall by a hair's breadth and passing safely through the lock gates. The people who had lined the harbour wall to help us tie up, cheered as all four boats passed safely into the outer basin, while the Harbour Master wiped his brow and mouthed a silent 'thank you' to the heavens, before closing the gates behind us.

Within an hour, a light breeze had sprung up, the fog had cleared and we found ourselves enjoying a cup of tea on deck under a clear, blue sky. The following weekend, we went to the chandlers and bought a new compass for the *Fiona*, but I resolved NEVER AGAIN to venture out in a pea-souper!" She tapped the page once more before closing the Log Book, but I had to ask,

"Grandma, what's a 'pea-souper'?"

"When I was a girl," she replied, "all manner of rubbish came out of the factory chimneys. To make things worse, most people burnt coal to heat their homes. The result was, that whenever it was foggy, the soot and sulphur in the air would cling to the mist and make it look like thick, yellowy-green, pea soup, so people called them 'pea-soupers'. I think that's why I've always preferred chicken broth!" she chuckled.

It must have been the mention of food, for at that moment, Dotty arched her back, stretched her paws and began to knead the rope mat.

Chapter 2

"All right, Missy," said Grandma. "One last time."

The little cat chirped with excitement as my grandmother opened the sail locker and retrieved a large keep net and a tiny, red life jacket with the words, 'SMALL DOG' written in black letters on one side. She was always very careful to make sure that Dotty was wearing her life jacket whenever she was near water, because although the cat loved to swim, she could grow tired very quickly, especially when the water was as cold as it was at this time of the year.

When my grandfather had found out how much Dotty liked to swim, he had set about trying to find a life jacket that was a good fit for her. Being a Bengal cat meant that she was strong and muscular with a long, sleek body and it proved difficult to find a life jacket that was designed for a cat, that would fit her well. One day, my grandmother spotted a little, red life jacket in a seaside junk shop. The words, 'SMALL DOG' were printed on the side. The shop owner had laughed when Grandma had arrived with a cat on a leash and had said,

"I think your cat's a bit confused, missus. Does she think she's a dog? Walks on a lead, swims in the sea. She doesn't even sound like a cat, more like a bird with a sore throat! Next, you'll be telling me that she fetches sticks!"

Grandma, always protective of her cat, answered,

"I haven't taught her to do that yet, as she wouldn't see any point in it, but she can do a 'High Five'."

The man had watched in amazement as the little cat had lifted her paw in response to Grandma's request for the greeting.

"Well I'll be ..." he exclaimed.

The man had been so impressed by Dotty that he had given her the life jacket, free of charge. Grandma thanked him and said that she would have to take the cat shopping with her more often.

SMALL DOG, as the life jacket became known, became a familiar sight to the crowds that gathered to watch Dotty swimming in the Old Harbour during the summer months.

"It is usually too chilly for her to swim at this time of year," Grandma explained as she tightened the harness around the little cat's body, "but today, the weather is fine, so ..."

Without finishing the sentence, she lowered Dotty over the side and watched happily as she swam backwards and forwards, up and down the inner basin. In the summer, the crowds that had gathered to watch the famous swimming cat, were so large that it had led to her winning a tourism award for encouraging people to visit the Old Harbour. Mr Williamson, a reporter for the local newspaper, the *Clarion*, had written an article about her. She had become known as 'The Salty Sea Cat' and was admired by all who saw her.

Since the season had changed and the warm summer days had given way to a damp and misty autumn, fewer people came regularly to witness her antics and today, only a handful of visitors watched from the dockside. They cheered and applauded, as she flattened her ears to keep out the water and thrust her whiskers forward to measure how close the level was to her nose. From time to time, she chirped like a 'bird with a sore throat', as her little legs moved like an old-fashioned paddle boat, propelling her swiftly through the water.

Bob and Blender had finished their photoshoot and stood watching Dotty's performance from the path above us. Bob smiled as he looked on, but as if she was jealous of anyone, or anything, receiving more attention than her, I heard Blender say loudly,

"What a stupid animal! How silly she looks doing that 'catty paddle'."

"I suppose that must be Blender," sighed Grandma with a shake of her head, adding in an equally loud voice, "There's only one stupid creature here, and it's not swimming at the moment," then muttering under her breath, she added, "but that could easily be arranged!"

Bob and Blender had just reached the gate above us and were about to come down the steps, when we saw Mr Robertson's car come to a halt on the other side of the dock.

He called across the inner basin, "Come on you two. We need to leave immediately. I've managed to book a table at the pizza restaurant next to the cinema. We'll just have enough time to eat there before the film starts."

 Bob had told me that his parents were eager to find as many things for Blender to do during her stay with them over half term, that would keep her out of the house for as long as possible. He had mentioned that they were going to see a film that evening, but his father had obviously found a way of extending his niece's absence from his home, for even longer.

I watched as they made their way back to the car, where Mr Robertson loaded Bob's bicycle onto the rack at the back. Blender waited until he had finished, tapping her foot impatiently until he held the door open for her to get into the back, while Bob took his place in the passenger seat. It might have been a trick of the light, but as they drove away, I was sure that I saw Blender look in our direction and stick out her tongue.

I followed the car with my eyes until it disappeared behind the row of trees at the corner of the road. When I turned away, I met Grandma's gaze.

"Don't let her bother you," she said. "She's nothing more than ... than..."

"A flibbertigibbet?" I offered.

"Exactly!" said Grandma, adding with a wink of her eye, "Whatever that may be."

As I climbed into bed that night, I took my log book from the shelf above it and slowly turned pages that were filled with my stories of sunny days and watery adventures. I was pleased that my grandmother had encouraged me to keep a record of my stay with her during the summer holidays earlier that year. It had been our way of sharing our exploits with my mother and Aunt Hattie. I never thought that it would also help to cheer *me* up.

"Still reading?" asked Grandma as she popped her head round my door to say goodnight. She sat on the edge of the bed and looked at my drawings and stories about the adventures we had shared and seeing the sadness in my eyes, said,

"What a time we had when we went 'Past the Town of Tribulation and Straight on to Derring Do'!"

We turned the pages, stopping in several places, as we remembered the small details of our exploits, some of which were dangerous, while others were amusing.

"I don't think there will be anything to write about in my log, this week," I said.

She kissed my forehead and said softly,

"We'll see. The one thing I've learnt about life, is that you never know what's round the next corner."

At that time, she could not have imagined how true her words would turn out to be.

Chapter 3

When we arrived at the Old Harbour on Sunday afternoon, it seemed deserted. The day had started, just as Grandma had predicted, shrouded in a thick fog that was slow to clear. It was not until after lunch that she announced that it was fine enough to leave *Graymalkin Cottage* and make our way over to the harbour.

"Take the key and go and get started with the rest of the packing," said Grandma as she parked the Land Rover. "I'll go and check on Billy O. This damp air is no good for him. I know he'll not take my advice, but I have to try. He'll say, 'Melissa, teeth placed before the tongue give the best advice' and then he'll carry on just as before."

I was about to ask Grandma what she meant, when I had a sudden picture of teeth clamped so tightly together that it would be impossible to say anything, and realised that it was Billy O's way of telling her to be quiet and not to 'mollycoddle' him … whatever that meant.

She had attached a lead to Dotty's harness and handed it to me with the firm instructions that I was to make sure it was securely tied to the cleat next to the coiled rope mat.

The inner basin lay in a dip between a tree-lined road on the right and a high bank on the left, providing protection for the boats that were moored there. Its sheltered location afforded a safe haven from the winds and waves that roared up the River Severn on stormy, winter nights. Today, because there was not a breath of wind, the low-lying fog had lingered here, long after it had left the rest of the Old Harbour. It was as if it had been trapped by the spiky branches that loomed above the water, reaching out like gnarled fingers and holding on to the grey mist, so tightly that it could not escape. Nothing in this strange, cotton-wool landscape around me seemed familiar. There was no birdsong, no gentle lapping of the water and for once, no scuttling and scurrying of the creatures that lived on the Rat Boat. Even so, I kept close to the bank and took care to step cautiously over the brambles and mooring lines that criss-crossed the path. I was almost level with the broken ladder that led on to the deck of the creaking hulk, when I was startled by a sudden movement on the deck. A shadowy figure moved quickly behind the wheelhouse, causing me to call out in surprise and alarm,

"Who's there?"

As I received no answer, I quickened my step, urging Dotty to keep pace with me. She had started to show an interest in exploring and was already clambering aboard the derelict boat, but a sharp tug on her leash and a few words of encouragement brought her back to the path. With great relief, we reached the *Fiona* and I picked up the little cat and hastily carried her on board.

The high, upturned bow of the Rat Boat stood a few feet above that of the *Fiona*, so a clear view of the wheelhouse and the weather deck was not possible from where I was standing near the stern of our boat. With trembling hands, I unlocked the padlock that secured the companion way and went below, taking Dotty with me. All the while, I watched for more activity on the neighbouring boat, but saw none. I made my way to the fore cabin and, standing on the raised berth, carefully opened the hatch above it, being careful to make as little noise as possible. From the open hatch, I now had a good view of the Rat Boat's deck as far as the wheelhouse. Despite the mist, I could see that something was moving: a something that was much larger than a rat or a squirrel. I was so busy trying to focus on whatever it was, that I completely forgot about Dotty until I saw her rush along the deck past me. On reaching the bow of the *Fiona*, she leapt high into the air and dug her strong claws into the wooden hull of the Rat Boat, before pulling herself on board. I reached out through the hatch in a vain attempt to grab the end of her leash as she passed, but she was too quick for me and it trailed behind her like a red ribbon, as she disappeared over the high bulwark of the old boat and was immediately lost from view.

At that moment, I saw another dark figure emerging from the fog and making its way along the path towards me.

"What are you up to?" called out the figure. I was relieved to recognise Bob's voice. He must have thought it strange to see my head sticking out of the hatch, like a jack-in-the-box with a broken spring. He looked even more puzzled when I shook my head, put my finger to my lips and pointed to the Rat Boat.

"Wait there," I whispered as loudly as I could.

I joined him on the pathway a few seconds later and told him what had happened.

"You're imagining it," he said. "There's no-one there."

No sooner had he spoken, than we heard,

"Scat, drat cat," from the other side of the wheelhouse and saw Dotty rushing towards us, chirping loudly and being pursued by an irate boy.

"Does that dreadful creature belong to you?" he shouted.

"She's not a dreadful creature, she's a cat!" I retaliated before I realised that it was a foolish thing to say, as a cat is a creature, after all.

As I cradled her in my arms, I almost had to agree that she was dreadful, because now that she felt safe, she flattened her ears, bared her fangs and hissed at him as if she was the most venomous of snakes.

He backed away, pressing himself against the wheelhouse door and it was then that I realised that, it was not that he disliked cats, but that he was actually afraid of them.

To my surprise, Bob addressed the boy by name,

"Don't worry, Ryan. She's had her lunch!" he laughed.

I took Dotty back to the *Fiona,* making sure that she was securely fastened to the cleat next to her rope mat.

"So our shadow is no more than a boy," I said as I sat near to her, stroking her gently until she was calm once more.

When I returned to the deck of the Rat Boat, Ryan seemed much more relaxed and was explaining to Bob why he was there and what he was doing.

"This was my great-uncle's boat," he said. "He was born near here, but he worked as a fisherman in Scotland for most of his life. When he retired, he bought this old fishing boat and sailed it all the way down the west coast, so that he could restore it. I think his plan had been to turn it into a houseboat and live on board, but he died suddenly and never got to finish it."

"Finish it," said Bob, "I don't think he even started it!"

Ryan looked dolefully at the rotting deck and stiff, oil-covered ropes. Here and there lay discarded pieces of broken machinery, empty oil cans and rusty winch cables.

"This isn't the worst of it," he added sadly. "You should see below."

The only way to enter the lower part of the boat was through a hatch in the deck, because the steps from the wheelhouse to the cabins had rotted away long ago. Ryan struggled to slide the hatch along its decaying, wooden runners.

"That's as far as it goes," he announced. He had managed to open it halfway, just enough for us to peer down into what would have once been the fish hold. I reeled backwards, my nose stinging from the sharp stench. It seemed that even the air was eager to escape its damp, dark prison, and surged upwards in a sudden rush.

"Phew," said Bob, holding his nose. "You're not going down there are you? It's full of rats."

"They'll soon make themselves scarce," replied Ryan with a new-found confidence. I thought it was strange that he was not afraid of rats, but had been terrified of a little pussy cat.

It was becoming more and more apparent that he expected us to go down into the hold with him.

"There's a ladder," he said when he noticed that I was staring down into the darkness with fear and loathing. "Well, at least there's a ladder for part of the way," he added, trying desperately to reassure me that climbing into a rat-infested cavern, while hanging on to a rotting piece of wood, suspended above a putrid pool, was the most natural thing in the world.

Thankfully at that moment, Grandma appeared on the path and said,

"What on earth do you think you're doing?"

I was tempted to say, 'Nothing', but as Grandma suspected that people always gave that reply when they were up to no good, I kept silent and allowed Bob to introduce Ryan.

"Your great-uncle liked to keep himself to himself," she said, when she had listened to his story, "but I met him once or twice when we visited our boat, and he told me about his plans to restore this old girl. Sadly, I think you're too late to rescue her now. There's so much water in the hold that the fact that she's resting against the side of the canal bank, must be the only thing that's stopping her from sinking."

"I was really excited when I heard that my great-uncle had left me a boat in his will. I thought it would be something like yours," he nodded in the direction of the *Fiona*. "What makes it worse," he continued, "is that he left me a letter."

At this point, he thrust a crumpled piece of paper towards Grandma, who having perched her reading glasses on the end of her nose, read the contents aloud.

"Dear Lad," she began.

"He always called me 'Lad'," explained Ryan. "I don't think he could remember my name."

Although I had not known him for very long, it seemed to me that Ryan's voice was always full of sadness and his face wore a constant expression of deep unhappiness. It was as if he always expected things to go wrong, whereas Grandma believed that things would always go right, if they knew that it was expected of them.

Grandma began again,

"Dear Lad, I am leaving my boat in your hands. There is much work to be done and it will be the greatest challenge of your life. Do not let me down."

The letter finished with details of the boat and where it could be found.

As Grandma handed the letter back, Ryan looked even more wretched and downcast than before.

"The one thing I've learnt about life is that you never know what's round the next corner," she gave her familiar words of encouragement, before adding cheerily, "Come over to the *Fiona* and have a cup of tea."

Even her kindness failed to lift his low spirits and he answered dolefully, "Thank you, but I need to finish off here, first. I'm making a list of everything I'll need, so that I can try to get some idea of how much everything is going to cost."

As Grandma, Bob and I made our way to the *Fiona*, I glanced back at Ryan, and watched as he stood in the middle of the deck and looked about him, despairing at the size of the task that he had been set.

On the pathway, Bob told me what he knew of Ryan.

"He's in my class at school," he said, "but I don't know him very well. To be honest, I don't think anybody knows him very well. He's sort of 'different', I suppose. He's not clever, he's not good at sports, his parents split up and he lives with his grandmother and she's not very well off, so his clothes are never cool. I don't think he has a single friend and because he's usually on his own, he gets picked on by people like Phil Renney and Dave Higgins."

I had met the two boys he mentioned, once before. The inner basin was fed by a canal, that in turn was fed by a small river. One day in the summer, Bob and I had been rowing along the canal, when two boys had appeared on the path above us. At the time, I had found it amusing when they had asked if I was Bob's girlfriend, and even funnier when he had replied that I was his sister. Later, I realised that this white lie was his way of avoiding being another victim of their bullying, and also his way of protecting me from their insults. When they had gone, Bob had told me that they were always looking for mischief and had been in trouble in the past. Miss Danvers had reported them to the police, when she had spotted them on one of the abandoned boats. Although they had not done any damage, the police told them that they were trespassing and went to see their parents. Phil's father was always drunk and could not have cared less, but Dave's father was a bully like his son, and beat him and grounded him for a week. After that, they were rarely seen in the Old Harbour and did their best to avoid Miss Danvers whenever they saw her in the town.

"At least Ryan must feel safe here," I said, feeling even more sorry for this boy, who seemed to have no-one.

I looked towards the Rat Boat and saw that it was deserted once more. Ryan had left without saying goodbye.

"Not used to kindness," Grandma observed.

That night, I took my log book from the shelf above my bed, turned to a clean page and wrote a new heading:

'HOW WE HELPED RAT BOAT RYAN'

Chapter 4

Monday was one of those perfect autumn days, when the sky was bright and, in Grandma's words, as 'blue as a pair of sailor's trousers'. If it had not been for the fact that the banks of the canal were lined with blackthorn and hawthorn, blackberries and elderberries and strands of wispy *Old Man's Beard* trailed from branch to branch, you could have easily believed that the day had been placed in the wrong season, being more suited to spring rather than to autumn.

Bob paddled slowly past the boats in the inner basin, under the swing bridge and into the canal. Swans swam alongside us now, seeming so much friendlier than they had done in the summer, when they had been eager to protect their young. The cygnets were losing their fluffy down and in its place, brown feathers covered their bodies and strong flight feathers were appearing along the edges of their wings. I sat at the back of the small boat and enjoyed the peace and quiet. There were no designer jackets, no hairdressing tips and no selfie sticks. The gentle lapping of the water was not disturbed by a single 'Cooee!'

The day had not started well. Earlier, Mr Robertson had deposited Bob and Blender at the Old Harbour and departed with his usual haste. My heart had sunk as I had watched them coming along the track that led to the *Fiona*. If Bob had intended going to his father's boat, the *Morning Star*, he would have taken the small, blue tender from the pontoon and rowed out to where the yacht was moored in the centre of the basin. Instead, I watched gloomily as they crossed the lock and took the cinder path above us, knowing that in a few minutes they would arrive at my grandmother's boat.

Unfortunately for me, today Blender seemed to be less interested in making Bob do exactly what she wanted and more intent on making me feel that I had just crawled out from under a stone and should return there without delay. As soon as she climbed on board, she sat down close to me. Very close to me, indeed. At first, she said nothing, but seemed to be inspecting the side of my head thoroughly. Then she spoke,

"You know, your hair would be all right with a few highlights and one or two extensions," she declared with an air of authority. Lifting the hair above her left ear, she continued,

"Look, I had mine done at Delorio's in London."

As I had no idea what or who a 'Delorio' was, I just smiled and nodded.

However, Grandma did not take kindly to Blender's suggestions about how my appearance could be improved.

"Megan is nine, not nineteen," she snapped, "and personally, I think her hair could not be any more beautiful than it is already. It would definitely not be improved by adding any such folderols!" she blurted out.

I sensed that now was not a good time to ask what a 'folderol' was, but the strangeness of the word seemed to stop Blender in her tracks for a few seconds, before she was on the attack once more.

"I would hate Megan to arrive at secondary school next year and feel ... 'different'. It's so easy to get left out."

I half expected to see smoke pouring out of Grandma's ears and when she spoke, she was barely able to hide the anger in her voice.

"I hope she is 'left out' by any idiot who is impressed by such ... such ...," she paused as she struggled to find a word that was strong enough to convey exactly what she thought of this empty-headed girl and I waited for the explosion of words that were bubbling away in her head. When they came, they were the most splendid words I could have imagined, even if I had no idea what half of them meant.

"... gewgaws, codswallop, fiddle-faddle and baloney," she shouted with such force that Blender moved away from me, and that was when she made her biggest mistake of all. In shuffling along the bench, she almost sat on Dotty, who chirped out a warning.

"Oh, move out of the way, fleabag!" she said, nudging the cat so hard that it fell onto the deck.

"FLEABAG," roared Grandma. "Fleabag indeed! My cat is probably far cleaner than you are with your stuck on rats' tails. Leave my boat IMMEDIATELY!" she shouted.

To me, Grandma was always kind and gentle and I was shocked by this outburst. Blender did not need to be told twice and tilting her chin upwards in an attempt to look superior, climbed off the boat and made her way along the path.

"I know when I'm not wanted," she muttered, when she was at a safe distance. She had ordered Bob to follow and insisted that he should row her across to the *Morning Star,* so that she could watch television on board, adding that,

"The *Fiona* is too much of an antique to have a television. It's so old," she had sneered, "that you probably have to use a pigeon to send a message."

Bob had given her a sharp look and hurried her along the path. As they reached the bottom of the steps that led back up to the track above us, he turned for a moment and, with an apologetic look, silently mouthed, "Sorry".

I had watched as he had rowed her across to the *Morning Star*'s mooring in the centre of the basin.

"I don't like the cut of her jib!" Grandma had nodded towards Blender, as the girl stepped onto the low platform on the stern of Bob's boat.

"What does that mean?" I asked, determined to understand at least some of my grandmother's strange sayings.

"A long time ago," she began, "different countries had different styles of jib sails. When sailors said that they didn't like the cut of another ship's jib, it usually meant that they didn't like the country that the ship came from, rather than the sail itself. After all, it would be silly to dislike a sail, wouldn't it?"

As with most of my grandmother's best sayings, this one conjured up a picture in my head and I smiled as I imagined Blender with a large triangular sail in the place where her nose should have been.

I think she had expected Bob to stay on the *Morning Star* with her, but I had been pleased to see him paddling back towards the *Fiona*. He signalled to me to walk along the pathway to the ladder, so that I could join him in the tender. I had become far more confident and could now board the small boat without causing it to pitch and roll as violently as I had done on my first attempts. Despite this, I still felt happier to climb down the metal ladder at the side of the basin, while Bob held tightly to its bottom rung.

"What about Blender?" I asked. "What if she wants to go ashore?"

"She'll be fine," replied Bob. "The *Morning Star*'s tender is tied to the starboard side. Although that girl is far too lazy to row herself anywhere!"

I had noticed that Bob seemed to prefer the small, wooden tender that was often tied to the pontoon. It was one of a number of such boats that belonged to the Yacht Club and could be used by anyone to get to and from their boats. The one he always chose was painted pale blue and had an old saucepan in the bottom, just in case you took on too much water and needed to bail it out. When I asked him why he liked this particular boat, he replied that he preferred it because it handled much better than the 'modern monstrosity', as he called the *Morning Star*'s tender. I had to agree that when I wasn't causing it to wobble with my unsteady boarding actions, this was a fine little boat.

"No airs and graces!" Grandma would say about it and I knew exactly what she meant.

Our journey came to an end when we were confronted by the thick wall of reeds that marked the modern day limit of the canal. I knew that it went on for a short distance beyond this point, but as it was choked with weeds further up, this had to be the limit of our voyage. With sadness, I remembered that our return journey would take us back to Blender. It was not just her selfishness and her unkindness that upset me: it was the way she made me feel that I was not as good as her, in every single way.

"Is she staying all week?" I asked, unable to hide how downhearted I felt.

"I hope not," said Bob. "Her dad's in a lot of trouble. He's lost all of his money and they're having to move from their grand house in the country to a smaller place in the town. Her ladyship was having such a hissy fit about it all, that her parents asked Dad if she could stay with us for a few days while they sort everything out."

"How few?" I asked.

The question went unanswered, for as we returned to the inner basin, we were faced with a commotion, the like of which I had never seen before and hope never to see again.

Grandma, close to tears, was rushing backwards and forwards up and down the path. Miss Danvers, who had returned to her mooring near the swing bridge, was standing on deck, scanning the horizon, the trees, and even the depths of the water with her father's binoculars.

Billy O was joining in whatever frantic game they were playing by shuffling along behind Grandma, wheezing like a pair of broken bellows. I knew that it was serious, because he was actually calling her by her *real* name.

"Now, now, Melissa," he said, trying to make her stand still for a moment. "Heave to and make fast!"

His pleas made no difference, as Grandma continued her frantic search, sometimes poking in the bushes that lined the path and sometimes peering on the decks of the derelict boats alongside.

I was trying to understand the reason for all this activity, when I realised that something, or someone, was missing from this scene: Dotty was nowhere in sight.

"This is serious," said Bob.

A police car had parked near to the pontoon and our old friend, P. C. Raines stepped out. He was one of the policemen who had helped us recover goods that had been stolen from boats in the Old Harbour during the summer holiday. I remembered how he had fallen into the canal while trying to retrieve a pair of binoculars belonging to Miss Danvers. His sergeant had said that he was, 'Wet by name and wet by nature', but we liked him, even if he was liable to have accidents from time to time.

As soon as Grandma saw us, she rushed to the edge of the path and said,

"Please say that she's with you and that it's all been a joke," she pleaded tearfully.

"A joke?" I questioned. "What do you mean?"

With a few wheezes and whistles, Billy O brandished a piece of paper in the air and cried out,

"It's the cat. She's been kidnapped!"

Chapter 5

When P. C. Raines reached the *Fiona*, we sat in the cockpit and listened as Grandma recounted the sorry tale.

"Meg and Bob had just started to row up towards the canal and I decided that a nice cup of tea and a couple of Ship's Biscuits would be in order. I went below into the galley and put the kettle on. As it whistled, I heard a single 'chirp' from Dotty. I called up to her to be patient, as I would feed her as soon as I had finished my tea. When I returned to the deck, her little rope mat was empty and in the place where she had been lying, I found that awful note."

Here she paused to pat the little rope mat, letting out a loud sob as she did so.

"Note?" asked P. C. Raines.

Billy O thrust a piece of yellowing paper under the policeman's nose.

"Keel hauling would be too good for 'em!" he muttered as he handed over the ransom note.

P. C. Raines read aloud the words that had been scrawled in capitals on the page,

"IF YOU WANT TO SEE YOUR CAT AGAIN, LEAVE £100 IN A PAPER BAG UNDER THE OLD OAK TREE IN THE LANE AT 6 O'CLOCK TOMORROW EVENING."

He paused and seemed reluctant to read the next part, but Grandma nodded and said quietly,

"Go on."

The young police officer cleared his throat and continued,

"OTHERWISE ... CAT MEAT."

I covered my mouth to hide the shock and dismay I felt. Bob, on the other hand was very calm and quiet. He seemed to be studying the note in great detail.

P. C. Raines had placed it in an evidence bag, but it was still clearly visible through its plastic covering. After a few moments, Bob spoke.

"The paper is very old," he observed. "Most of it has turned yellow, but across the one side there's a faint red box with some writing on it. It looks as if someone was in a hurry when they tore it out, because one corner is missing,"

Everyone crowded round to peer more closely at the page, making it impossible for anyone to see anything. P. C. Raines took control.

"Stand back there!" he said as he lifted the page to the sunlight.

"Well I'm flabbergasted," chuckled Billy O. "It looks as if that piece of paper has been keeping close company with a newspaper that hasn't been published for nigh on forty years."

At the centre of the faint, red square, we could just make out the outline of some white lettering. As we turned our heads this way and that in an attempt to read the words, Billy O traced each letter with his finger, reading aloud as he did so,

"D-A-I-L-Y S-K-E-T-C-H," then putting it all together he said triumphantly, "The Daily Sketch! Find that and you'll soon have the blackguard in the brig!"

I didn't ask what he meant, but understood that if we found the newspaper, it would lead to the capture of the kidnapper.

The light was beginning to fade and we decided to go home and resume our search in the morning. With great reluctance, Grandma was persuaded to return to *Graymalkin Cottage*.

I think none of us slept at all on that night. At ten o'clock, I heard my grandmother pacing back and forth in her room; at midnight, I heard her calling the cat's name in the garden; at two o'clock, I heard her making tea in the kitchen; at four o'clock, I heard the printer whirring away as it churned out 'Missing Cat' posters and at six o'clock, she was back in the garden.

We sat in silence as we ate breakfast, although it would have been more accurate to say that Grandma *didn't* eat breakfast. Instead, she shuffled her food around the plate, before scooping it into the bin. It was a bleary-eyed pair that arrived at the Old Harbour that morning, but I was surprised to see that we were not the first there. Billy O was not in his usual place on Watch, but could be seen scouring the hedgerows alongside the moorings. He was accompanied by Bob, who was peering into the water at the edge of the path.

For the rest of the day, we searched everywhere in the Old Harbour and when we had finished, we searched again. Grandma pinned up the posters she had made on every tree and post she could find. When she ran out of places close by, she drove down to the town and put up more there.

The lady with the Jack Russell that had once frightened Dotty so much that she had almost jumped into the dock, had heard what had happened and came to help.

"The dog will track her down," she said confidently, but all he found was a half-eaten sausage roll that had been thrown into the bushes.

On Grandma's return, I thought that her handbag had grown in size, until I realised that, while she had been in town, she had taken the opportunity to visit the bank and withdraw the ransom money, despite P. C. Raines telling her not to do so.

Up until this point, I had felt upset about Dotty's disappearance, but now I felt angry. Anyone who knew her, would realise that Grandma was not a rich person and a hundred pounds was a lot of money for her to lose.

"We've *got* to do something!" I said to Bob, as we made one final search of the canal bank.

"But what?" asked Bob.

"I don't know … yet."

On the other side of the harbour, Grandma was still putting up posters, asking people to contact her if they knew anything about the kidnap of Dotty Cat. Occasionally, people visiting the Old Harbour, walking their dogs or working on their boats would stop to talk to her. They would shake their heads sadly as they listened to the unhappy fate of the little cat. After all, she had brought so much joy and happiness to all who had watched her swimming during the summer.

Chapter 6

"I think we should go and help Grandma," I said to Bob as we closed the *Fiona*'s hatches. "She's so lost without Dotty." I felt close to tears myself, as I watched my grandmother trying everything she could in order to solve the crime. She would be dreading a second night without her 'flibbertigibbet', especially as the deadline for the payment of the ransom was approaching.

I followed Bob along the towpath that led to the steps and the track above. As we passed alongside the Rat Boat, he stopped suddenly. He stood rooted to the spot for a moment and gazed in amazement at the wheelhouse of the derelict hulk. Without saying a word, he clambered on board and, shielding his eyes from the low rays of the setting sun, peered in at the grimy widow. The hinges were so badly rusted, that it was no longer possible to close the door of the wheelhouse properly. It seemed that it had been opened recently, leaving a gap that was just big enough for the breeze to squeeze through and rustle the papers on the shelf beneath the window. One piece in particular was being thrown up by the draught and was flapping against the glass. With a great effort, Bob managed to lift the door and pull it open wide enough to allow him to enter the cabin.

"Yes," he cried. "Got you!" and picking up the page turned it towards me so that I could see the bright, red banner across the top. It read,

Daily Sketch

At first, I had no idea why he was so pleased with his find, then slowly the memory of what Billy O had told us crept into my mind. The ransom note had been written on paper that had been lying close to a copy of the *Daily Sketch*, a newspaper that had not been printed since the 1970s. Forgetting my fear of the Rat Boat, I climbed the rickety, wooden ladder onto the deck and joined Bob in the wheelhouse. The breeze had disturbed some of the papers on the shelf, but we soon found what we were looking for. At the far end, lay a pad of blank paper, yellowed with age and sunlight. However, the top page seemed paler than the rest, having been protected until recently by a sheet above it. The missing piece of paper had been torn out so hastily that a jagged corner remained on the left hand side.

"Do you remember how the ransom note had a corner missing?" asked Bob. He ran his finger across the top of the pad. "I bet it would fit this like a jigsaw."

At that moment, the wind dropped and all was still. It was then that we heard it: a chirp, faint at first, but growing louder as we started to call out the little cat's name.

"It's coming from beneath us," said Bob, rushing from the wheelhouse towards the deck hatch.

It was dusk and as we peered into the open hatch, the inside of the hold was already in total darkness. Undaunted, Bob started to climb down the ladder, but I held onto his arm. Memories of the black, oily waters at the bottom of the boat made me cry out,

"Stop! It's too dangerous. I'll go and get a torch from the *Fiona*. Wait until I get back ... Promise?"

Bob nodded in agreement and I left him sitting on the top rung of the ladder. As I went into the *Fiona*'s cabin, I could hear Bob talking to the Dotty, reassuring her that we would be with her soon.

I found the torch in the compartment under the radio and was about to leave when I decided that some protection for our feet might be a good idea. My dread of the rats that I had seen swimming in the dark waters around the boat, was almost greater than the need to rescue Dotty. I found what I was looking for in the wet weather locker: a pair of my grandfather's wellingtons for Bob, together with my own red boots. A collection of sailing gloves lay alongside the boots and I chose a pair that looked as if they were more suited to wear on a motor bike than on a boat. They were made from a waterproof fabric and had a strap at the wrist. I was determined that not a drop of that dark water would touch me.

Feeling that we were now well prepared to carry out a rescue from a rat-infested wreck, I made my way back to the Rat Boat, but my confidence soon turned to despair, when I arrived to find the deck empty. I switched on the torch and peering over the edge of the hatch, followed the path of the beam as it swept the hold below.

"Bob," I called out, "where are you?"

I was relieved to hear his voice: "It's okay," he said, "I didn't have to get my feet wet after all. Shine the torch to the left and you'll see a ledge. I think they must have used it to walk along so that they could check the cargo when it was piled high."

I hardly wanted to ask the next question, "Dotty ... is she okay?" I asked falteringly.

"You'd better ask her," came the reply.

I called out her name and was reassured by a loud chirp when she recognised my voice. I slipped the torch's lanyard over my wrist and pulled on my red boots, just in case I had to wade in the murky waters below me. Holding tightly to the ladder, I lowered myself down into the darkness, a rung at a time. As I reached the last step above the water's surface, I lifted the torch so that I could see the ledge.

"Hold onto the side of the ladder with one hand and reach out as far as you can with the other." Bob's voice from the shadows gave me encouragement. "You'll find the edge of what must have been an old doorway. Hold onto it and pull yourself onto the ledge."

Despite the fact that my hands were buried in sailing gloves that were at least two sizes too large for me, it was easier than I thought, and soon I found myself on a narrow platform. Shining the torch along its length, I could see Bob at the far end of it. To my great relief, Dotty was cradled in his arms.

"We'll soon have you back home," he comforted the little cat, stroking her gently.

Before long, I was kneeling next to Bob, speaking soothingly to Dotty and finding myself rewarded with loud chirps.

"I can't believe that Rat Boat Ryan has done something so cruel. He must be desperate for the money to repair this old boat," I said.

I thought about how Dotty had been kept in the darkness, surrounded by rats and bilge water and felt angry about what had been done to her.

"What time is it?" Bob asked.

I shone the torch onto my wristwatch and was horrified to see that it was almost six o'clock.

"The deadline!" I cried out. "We must reach Grandma before she hands over the ransom."

Without delay, we started back along the ledge. Bob led the way with the cat in his arms, while I used the torch to light our way. We had reached halfway, when the boat swayed slightly and Bob stopped, signalling for me to do likewise.

"Shh!" he whispered. "Listen. There's somebody on the deck. It must be the kidnapper!"

I switched off the torch and stood stock-still, hardly daring to breath, as a light from the hatch raked the darkness below.

"You down there," said a voice from the top of the ladder. "What are you doing on my boat?"

The light was in my eyes, but I recognised the voice: it was Rat Boat Ryan.

I could not contain my anger and shouted, "And what are *you* doing with my cat?"

"And what's your cat doing on *my* boat?" he retaliated.

"She's here because *you* kidnapped her!" I blurted out.

"What? You must be joking. I prefer to keep well away from cats. Wouldn't touch one if you paid me."

"I thought paying him was the idea," I mumbled to Bob, as I remembered the ransom demand for one hundred pounds.

Bob knew that we were at a disadvantage, trapped down in the hold, so he said,

"Well, help us to get her out of here and we'll talk about it on deck."

I wanted to get out of the hold as soon as possible, as I had started to hear faint scratching noises and Dotty had begun to take an interest in something small and furry behind us.

Rat Boat Ryan was now half way down the ladder and had just extended his hand to help us from the ledge, when we all stopped and listened, as more footsteps were heard on the deck above.

"Switch off the torch!" whispered Bob, urgently.

We saw another figure silhouetted against the evening sky above the hatch and remained motionless as it started to climb down the ladder.

"This will be your last meal, you disgusting creature ... and if the ransom is not paid, I mean LAST!"

"BLENDER!" I yelled, flicking the switch of my torch and dazzling the kidnapper.

She was so shocked by the suddenness of my shout and the brightness of the light in her eyes, that she lost her footing and fell from the ladder into the oily, rat-infested water at the bottom of the hold.

She flapped and floundered like a fish out of water, except for the fact that she was *in* the water. Bob and Rat Boat Ryan tried to haul her onto the ledge, but she shrugged off their offers of help and remained where she was. As if proof of Blender's guilt, if any was needed, Dotty spat and hissed at her.

More footsteps were heard above us, but this time they were accompanied by a whistling wheeze that sounded like a punctured balloon.

"Man overboard!" wheezed Billy O as he held his old-fashioned storm lantern above the hatch. It flooded the hold with a warm glow and sent the rats scurrying back to their dark corners.

As usual, he had the knack of making light of even the worst situation and I began to chuckle as I took in the scene: there was Ryan, hanging by one arm to the ladder and Bob, cradling the little cat, who was convinced that it was her ferocious reputation that had sent the rats scampering for cover, and was now struggling to free herself from Bob's grip so that she could finish the job. Right at the centre of all of this was the best sight of all: Blender stood up to her knees in oily water. Her earlier fall had resulted in her being covered from top to toe in black slime that now dripped from her highlighted hair and onto her designer jacket.

"More like girl IN board!" I laughed.

"It's no laughing matter," pouted Blender. "My jacket is ruined and what's worse is that I've broken a finger nail!"

This brought more wheezing and laughter from Billy O, who said, "Broken a finger nail? You'll be lucky if you're not keel hauled for this!"

We did not know what keel hauling was, but it sounded as if it would be quite unpleasant.

"Come on you bilge rats," he added. "Let's heave you out and then we can decide what's to be done."

Bob went first so that he could pass Dotty up to Billy O on deck, then I followed. When I was half way up the ladder, the boat rocked again and Rat Boat Ryan cried out in desperation,

"Cripes, any more passengers and my poor old boat will sink!"

As I came onto the deck, two people were standing next to Billy O and I was relieved to see that Grandma was one of them. The other was P. C. Raines. He looked down into the water at the bottom of the boat and was pleased that someone else had got wet on this occasion. Rat Boat Ryan was the last to come up onto the deck, having made sure that Blender was safely on the ladder. Bob offered her his hand as she climbed onto the deck, but she ignored him, pushing him away and trying to look as dignified as anyone could do with slimy water dripping from the end of their nose.

Grandma held Dotty in her arms and stroked her gently, speaking soothingly while she examined the little cat for signs of injury. After a few minutes, she proclaimed her to be in good health, and that she was, in fact,

"Ship-shape and ..."

Bob and I, used to her strange sayings, joined in with a chorus of, "... Bristol fashion," which amused her greatly.

It was the first time I had seen her smile in two days.

One person who did not look amused was P. C. Raines, who confessed to being at a loss about what to do with Blender. He had taken down her name and address, but said that because of her age, an appropriate adult would have to accompany her to the Police Station.

"Don't look at me," said Grandma. "I want nothing more to do with the malicious madam!"

Billy O shook his head, "And that goes for me too. Delinquent dog's body! Chuck her in the chokey!"

If the situation had not been so serious, I think I would have exploded into fits of giggles. I didn't even think that it was the right moment to ask what a 'dog's body' was or indeed where the 'chokey' could be .

I think that Grandma was so pleased to have Dotty back safely, that she would have suggested that Blender got away with a ticking off, but P. C. Raines was quite clear,

"The law says that a serious crime has been committed and must be dealt with in a court of justice," and putting on his deepest, most official sounding voice, added, "Kidnap and demanding a ransom is an offence punishable by imprisonment!"

For a few seconds, a silence fell over the deck of the Rat Boat until finally, the reality of the situation dawned on Blender and she let out a wail, so loud that it would have rivalled the *Fiona*'s foghorn.

"Now, now Miss," said P. C. Raines and stepping forward to comfort the distraught girl, skidded on the pool of slime that had accumulated around her feet. In an attempt to steady himself, he made a frantic grab at Blender's sleeve, only succeeding in taking both of them over the broken rail at the side of the boat and into the water below.

Quickly, Billy O seized the lifebelt from the side of the wheelhouse and holding onto the line, cast it into the water. His aim was so good, that it narrowly missed Blender, sending more water over her head.

"Oh, oh," laughed Billy O, "it looks like the rats are leaving the sinking ship!"

We watched as two or three of Blender's hair extensions floated off across the basin.

"Well, at least it's washed the slime off!" he chuckled.

He was hauling the lifebelt towards the boat and had almost reached the side when he stopped, looked down into the water and said,

"Well, I'll be beached on a barnacle!"

He was brought sharply back to reality by Blender, who was spluttering and thrashing about, but before he started to pull her in again, I heard him mutter,

"The *Red Skye*!"

Chapter 7

When I opened my log book later that day, my cheeks
burned with shame as I read the title that I had written
two days before:

'HOW WE HELPED RAT BOAT RYAN'.

I felt embarrassed as I remembered how I had accused
him of being the kidnapper. To make matters worse,
instead of helping him to repair his boat, the bulwark
now had a new hole in it, where P. C. Raines and
Blender had collided with it as they had skidded
overboard.

That night, my dreams quickly turned to nightmares, as
my mind jumbled all of the recent events together and
created something truly terrifying. I saw myself trapped
in the hold of the Rat Boat, surrounded by rodents that
were the size of dogs. The only thing I had to defend
myself with, was a large, keep net like the one that
Grandma always used to scoop Dotty from the water. I

swung it to and fro in an attempt to keep the rats at bay. In my dream, the hatch above me opened suddenly and a blaze of light, like the brightest sunset I had ever seen, lit up the darkness. Two faces were silhouetted against the orange glow and I reached up, pleading for them to help me out. Instead, they laughed loudly and taunted me with the words, 'Red sky, red sky', which they chanted over and over again. I continued to swing the net in a wide arc around me, but one rat, braver than the rest, leapt forward. I felt its weight pressing on my chest and its wet nose on my face, causing me to fall backwards.

"Red sky!" I cried out so loudly that I woke myself up and was surprised to find Dotty sitting on my chest, her wet nose pressed against mine and her long tail swishing backwards and forwards in a wide arc.

The bedroom light flicked on and I saw Grandma standing in the doorway.

"What's all the noise about?" she asked.

I told her about my nightmare and she suggested that we have a warm, milky drink in the kitchen, then come back to bed and try to get some sleep, as it was only three o'clock in the morning.

As we sipped our milk, I asked, "Why did Billy O say 'red sky' when we were he was pulling the lifebelt back to the side of the Rat Boat?"

"Did he dear? I didn't hear him, but if you say so," she yawned.

Obviously this was not a good time to ask questions, so I finished my drink and, after I had apologised for disturbing everyone's rest, made my way back to bed. For the remainder of the night, I slept peacefully, but when I awoke the next morning, I was determined to ask the same question of Billy O.

I was pleased to be greeted by a blue sky, not a red one, when I drew back the curtains, and the promise of another fine day. I was delighted when Grandma said that we would spend the whole day at the boat.

"We need to make up for the time we've lost because of that madam's misdeeds," she said. "If we can finish packing today, then tomorrow you can help me to put everything into storage."

I tried not to look too disappointed by the fact that once the contents of the *Fiona* had been packed away and carried back to *Graymalkin Cottage*, our reason to visit the Old Harbour would no longer exist. I was determined to make the most of my last opportunity to see my friends there. As it turned out, I need not have worried, because although neither Grandma nor I knew it at the time, there would be little opportunity to finish the packing.

Our journey to the Old Harbour took us along a road that ran close to the inner basin at one point, and from where, the boats moored across the water, were clearly visible. The *Fiona*'s blue hull was now in view: to her stern lay a motor cruiser called the *Mechanical Ferret*, while the Rat Boat was moored off her bow. The boats on either side of ours were no longer used, and so a peaceful, tranquil scene usually greeted us on the last part of our journey. However, today the Rat Boat seemed to be a hive of activity. Before it was lost from view behind the trees along the roadside, I had been able to recognise Rat Boat Ryan, Billy O and two other men, both of whom seemed to be hanging over the side and peering into the water.

Once we had parked, I was so impatient to find out what was happening, that I left Grandma behind and set off at such a pace across the lock, up the cinder track, through the gate, down the steps and along the path, that when I arrived at the Rat Boat, I was too breathless to speak.

I did not need to speak, because I was greeted by Billy O, whose first words left me speechless.

"Good morning, gran'daughter and welcome aboard the *Red Skye*!"

Memories of my nightmare flooded back and I stood staring in disbelief.

"Don't stand there gaping like a guppy," he said. "Come and meet this fine old lady!" Grandma had caught up with me and the two of us accepted Billy O's invitation to come aboard.

The two men I had seen from across the road, seemed to have finished hanging over the side of the boat and had gone below. They now emerged through the hatchway from the hold, carrying clipboards, on which they were busily making a series of ticks and hastily scribbled notes. They moved to the bow of the boat and were engaged in a deep and private conversation, which involved a great deal of head scratching, pointing and nodding. While their discussion was taking place, Billy O and Rat Boat Ryan told me about the events of the past few hours.

"I wasn't sure at first," Billy O said, "but a memory kept rattling around this old brain of mine and then just as the Chief Steward was serving my Ship's Stew, it popped out. I frightened the life out of her by leaping up, hammering the table with my fist and shouting out, 'The *Red Skye*'. Well, she was convinced that I had lost my wits and was tempted to call a doctor. She watched in amazement, when I rushed from the room and started sorting through the books and papers in my desk, as if a force nine gale was blowing them to port and starboard, until finally I found it." Here, he paused and waved a dog-eared copy of a book with the title, *Herring Fishing in the Inner Hebrides*.

I had no idea how a small, tattered book could be the cause of so much excitement, and seeing the blank expression on my face, he went on to explain,

"As a young sailor, I spent some time in Scotland. The Isle of Skye was one of my favourite places to visit, but it was going through a difficult time. Herring fishing had provided the people who lived there with good employment for many years. The fish were so important to them that they called them 'silver darlings', but too many fish were caught and eventually, fewer and fewer were found in the waters around the islands, each year. Boats that had been built to catch the herring were called ring netters. With few fish to catch, they lay idle or were sold off. Some were converted to catch scallops or other fish, but eventually most became derelict. The *Skye Boats* were some of those that were lost," he broke off to explain. "They were called the *Skye Boats*, not only because they fished the waters around the Isle of Skye, but also because of their names. There were five of them originally: the *Blue Skye*, the *Dark Skye*, the *Summer Skye*, the *Cloudy Skye* and ... the *Red Skye*."

He opened his book to a full page, black and white photograph of five boats. The caption beneath it told me that it was taken in Portree Harbour on the Isle of Skye in 1950. The boat nearest to the camera had an outline that had become familiar to me during my visits to the *Fiona*. On each visit, I had looked up at the wheelhouse and the hawse hole, like an unblinking eye on the high prow, but the lettering beneath, so clearly visible in the picture, had been long lost. In the photograph standing out boldly against the black hull was written the name, '*Red Skye*'.

"*This* is the *Red Skye*?" I asked in surprise.

"Yes, and we're just in time!" said a voice from behind me. The two men had finished their work and were now ready to share their findings. As the four of us listened, I noticed how anxious Ryan looked and hoped, for his sake that the news would be good.

Billy O introduced the two men as Brian Wright of 'National Historic Ships UK' and Alex Dunbarry from the 'Scottish Fisheries Museum'.

"She ticks a lot of boxes," began Mr Wright. He went on to list how the *Red Skye* met the standards they set in helping them to decide if a ship or a boat was important enough to be included on the National Register of Historic Vessels.

"She's more than fifty years old," he made an invisible tick in the air with his pen.

"She was built and worked in the UK."

Another invisible tick.

"She's more than thirty-three feet in length."

Tick.

Here he paused and drew a deep breath.

"For us to take her on, she needs to be in a fairly good condition..."

We all held our breath as memories of the deep water in the hold and wood, so rotten that it had failed to stop P. C. Raines and Blender from falling overboard, came back.

"... and I'm pleased to announce that I can tick that box too. Just about!"

Mr Dunbarry explained further,

"The *Red Skye* is a reminder of how important herring fishing was to the people of Scotland and we would like to buy her for our museum," he paused and looked at Ryan, "if the owner is agreeable, that is."

Billy O chuckled, "The lad's lost his cabin colour, so I think you have your answer."

One look at Ryan told us all we needed to know. His pale face now seemed to shine and his features had been transformed by a broad smile that almost reached from ear to ear.

"Yes," he said without the slightest hesitation. "Yes!"

Mr Wright smiled and said that the first question he was usually asked was, 'How much?'.

"We don't have a bottomless purse," cautioned Mr Dunbarry, " and the cost of repair and restoration will be quite high, but we'll make you a fair enough offer."

"As long as I have enough to buy a boat like the *Fiona*, I don't mind," said Ryan. Grandma glowed with pride to think that her 'Old Girl', as my grandfather used to call the boat, was so admired by others.

For the rest of the morning, plans were laid for moving the *Red Skye* from her mooring. Mr Wight's inspection had revealed that the water in the hold was the result of the hull coming to rest on a broken stone in the harbour wall, just below the waterline. Over time, slight movements of the wooden hull against the stone had worn a hole in it. A temporary repair would need to be made and the hold pumped dry before any journey could be undertaken.

When Bob arrived later that morning, he was met by four very excited people. The story tumbled out as each of us added something, until Bob confessed that his head was spinning.

"What I don't understand," he said, "Is how Mr Wright and Mr Dunbarry found out about the *Red Skye*."

"I know that someone here will never blow his own trumpet," said Grandma, "So I will do it for him. The credit must go to Captain O'Donnell."

Billy O told us that after he had found the picture in his book, he had telephoned an old friend on the Isle of Skye, who remembered the *Red Skye* and even remembered Ryan's great-uncle buying her.

"Then I thought I had hit a dead end," Billy O shook his head sadly. "I rang the contact he had given me for the Museum, only to be told that the man I needed to speak to had gone to London for a meeting, and would not be returning to Scotland for several days. It was then that we had our greatest stroke of luck, because I was also told that his meeting was with none other, than an old friend of mine, Brian Wright. I rang Brian and he told me that he and Mr Dunbarry would be travelling to Bristol on the following morning, but could make a small detour and call at the Old Harbour on their way."

"I think they might be late for that meeting," said Grandma, nodding towards the two men who, excited by their find, had completely forgotten that they should have been somewhere else.

Chapter 8

On Thursday morning, a large crowd gathered on the dockside to watch the first stage in the rescue of the *Red Skye*. By mid-morning, two divers, who had been sent into the water to assess the damage, had found the hole and had set about making a temporary repair. By lunchtime, a large pump that had arrived from Bristol by boat, had been brought through the lock and now lay alongside the *Red Skye*.

Bob and I had an excellent view from our front row seat on the bow of the *Fiona*, from where we were able to watch the whole operation. Grandma was enjoying herself being busy and useful, and would pass by from time to time, carrying cups of tea and bacon sandwiches to the workers on the deck of the *Red Skye*, where Billy O was 'supervising'.

"More like putting his oar in," my grandmother remarked.

When she had returned from her last visit, I asked, "How soon will we know if it's going to float or …"

They're setting the pump up now, so we'll soon know if the repair has been successful," she said.

I did not want to think about the possibility of the boat sinking when they moved her away from the berth that she had occupied for so long, and I hoped for Ryan's sake that it would not be the case. Occasionally during the morning, his head had appeared above us and he would call down, telling us about the progress that had been made and what was going to happen next, then he would return to pacing the deck, anxiously.

P. C. Raines joined us just before one o'clock. He had come to have, 'a private word' with Grandma and I suspected that it was something to do with Blender. Instead of leaving after he had spoken to her, he came and sat with us on deck to watch the activity, while we told him everything that was being done to make the boat watertight.

"I hear they're hoping to try and take her across to Sharpness on the high tide at five o'clock," he said.

"The sun sets at about six o'clock, so they should just about manage to tow her in by then. It's only a mile, so she should make it."

At that moment, Ryan appeared on the *Red Skye*'s prow and called down to us,

"Mr Wright has suggested that you move to the stern, as they're about to start pumping and the force of the water might create a few waves. It could get a bit rocky on the bow."

We could see two large, black pipes trailing over the side of his boat and although we would have liked to stay where we were, as we would have had a good view of the water gushing out, we thought it best to watch from a safe distance. We stood up and had started to make our way to the stern, when we heard a murmur, then a gurgle, then a loud splash, as the sludge from the hold hit the water beside us with such force, that the pipe nearest to our bow looped and writhed like a giant snake.

I looked back to where we had been sitting and shook my head in disbelief,

"Not again," I said. "He's definitely 'wet by name and wet by nature'."

As Bob and I had made our way to the stern, we had assumed that P. C. Raines was following us, but he had remained just a little too long to talk to Ryan and, as a result, had been soaked from head to foot by the water from the wriggling pipe.

Fortunately, one of the divers had a spare set of dry clothes and, once again P. C. Raines found himself shivering in the cockpit of the *Fiona*, while Grandma served him tea and bacon sandwiches. Despite his drenching, like the rest of us, he was determined to stay until the end of the job.

By two o'clock, Mr Wright called out that the hold had been emptied and the repair seemed to be secure. The *Red Skye* no longer had a working engine, so the boat that had carried the pump, now took on a new role: it was to be the tug that would tow the old boat across the River Severn to Sharpness. The plan was to work on her there, so that she would be to seaworthy enough to make the long journey back to Scotland in the spring.

The lines that had kept her securely moored for so long, were now untied and reattached to the tugboat. We heard Mr Wright order everyone off the *Red Skye* and knew that the moment we had waited for, had finally arrived. Billy O and Ryan joined us on the *Fiona*, none of us scarcely daring to breathe as the wooden boat creaked and scraped away from her mooring and into the middle of the basin. At first she lurched and swayed unsteadily, until at last she lay still. Having made one final check of the hold, Mr Wright's thumbs up sign acted as a signal for the onlookers to cheer and applaud.

The tugboat manoeuvred the old trawler into the lock and we waited until the water had risen high enough to allow them to pass through. We now took up our position near to Billy O's Watch on the pier head. The Harbour Master told us that the Coastguard had made sure that no large ships would be coming into the port, guaranteeing a clear passage for the *Red Skye*. The sun was now so low in the sky, that it tipped the river's tiny wavelets in gold. It was as if it was putting on its own welcome display for a very special old lady.

At five o'clock the Harbour Master opened the lock gates that stood between the Old Harbour and the River Severn and, with mixed emotions, I watched as the *Red Skye* passed through. I shielded my eyes so that I would be able to see her safely across the river and into port on the other side. As the setting sun turned the river red, she arrived at her destination.

Billy O gave a deep sigh and said,

"Let's hope her sunset years are just as beautiful."

He took out his handkerchief, blew his nose and wiped a tear from his eye.

"Must be catching a cold," he said.

Chapter 9

While I was completing my log later that evening, Grandma came in to see me. I no longer felt guilty when I read the heading, 'HOW WE HELPED RAT BOAT RYAN', as everything had turned out well for him. I had filled the page with the story of the *Red Skye* and the people I had met that day. I was most proud of the picture I had drawn at the end of my story: It showed the old boat sailing across to Sharpness at sunset.

Grandma read what I had written and when she had finished, instead of kissing me goodnight as she usually did, seemed reluctant to leave. She sat on the edge of the bed and spoke slowly and quietly.

"I've reached a decision," she said. "I have told P. C. Raines that I don't want the matter with Blender to go any further. I hope she's had a big enough shock to make her change her ways. I understand that she goes home on Saturday and he's made it clear to her, that she's to go nowhere near to the Old Harbour before then. Let's hope she's learnt her lesson and will try to be a better person from now on."

I was tempted to use one of Grandma's favourite sayings, 'A leopard cannot change its spots', but thought better of it.

"You know," she continued, "you should never feel that people like her are better than you, because you have something that she will never have," she paused for a moment as if she wanted to make sure that I really understood what she was about to say, "Kindness," she said, "that is the most important thing."

I lay awake for a while and thought about her words.

Tomorrow was Friday, my last chance to spend the day with my friends at the Old Harbour, as my mother would be returning from holiday and intended to collect me on Saturday morning. At least my last day would be untroubled by Blender and her unkindness and I would be able to enjoy the company of people I liked … or so I thought.

"Let's get this job finished," said Grandma, as her old Land Rover rattled down the lane from *Graymalkin Cottage*, next morning. "It's never taken so long to pack up one small boat before. Every time we start, we have to stop! What with kidnappers and rats and wet policemen ..."

I was not sure that our intention to finish packing up the contents of the Fiona would go to plan, because the first sight to meet our eyes was that of Bob and Billy O,who appeared to be searching the path at the side of the pontoon.

"Thieves," wheezed Billy O, when we joined them. "Some folk are as crooked as a Corsair! Some cunning cove has pinched the tender, although I'm at a loss to know what they would want with that leaky old thing."

"Is anything else missing?" asked Grandma.

"That's the odd thing," said Bob. "There are plenty of much more valuable things around here, but nothing else seems to have been touched. It's not even the best boat."

It may have been true that it was not the best boat, but it was the one that Bob always chose from the row of small tenders that were tied up near to the pontoon.

"Perhaps someone has used it to row out to their boat," I suggested, "After all, that's what it's for!"

Some of the larger yachts were moored in the centre of the basin and could only be reached by rowing out to them. The Yacht Club kept several tenders on the pontoon for that purpose.

"We've considered that," replied Bob, "But there's no-one else here."

All the time we had been talking, Dotty had been so anxious to leave the pontoon, that she had started to chirp loudly and tugged so hard on her leash, that she almost pulled me over.

"Have you been up as far as the canal? It could have broken loose and drifted there," said Grandma. Bob thought that it would be unlikely, as wind and rain rarely raised so much as a ripple in the inner basin. He agreed to go and have a look, just in case someone had not fastened the little boat securely to the large iron ring on the pontoon when they had last used it.

"Perhaps you would like to take this flibbertigibbet with you." Grandma suggested as no amount of fussing seemed to be able to calm the cat. We were going to be close to water, so SMALL DOG was wrapped around Dotty's body. As she was tightening the harness, my grandmother warned us that under no circumstances was the cat to go into the water. The life jacket was a precaution just in case she fell in, not an invitation to swim.

We took the roadway as far as the swing bring at the end of the inner basin. I looked across the water to the row of boats moored on the other side. This was the view I always enjoyed whenever we arrived by car: I would look for the *Fiona*'s bright blue hull , standing out against the dense brush and brambles behind her.

"It doesn't look the same now that the Rat Boat," I stopped for a moment and corrected myself, " i mean, the *Red Skye* isn't there anymore. It's just like when you lose one of your front teeth."

"The difference is, a new tooth will sometimes grow in the gap," laughed Bob. "I don't think another *Red Skye* will pop up."

We reached the swing bridge and stood in the centre, so that we had a clear view up the canal in front of us and down the inner basin behind. We could see Grandma walking down the steps to boat, with Billy O puffing and blowing behind her. We waved to them and called out that there was no sign of the tender.

Instead of retracing our steps along the roadway, we continued to the far end of the bridge, where a path led to the high track that ran between the River Severn to our right and the inner basin to the left. The tide was rising rapidly and we watched as it raced past us.

"I'm glad we're up here," said Bob. "There's a big Bore in about about half an hour and that water is in one mighty hurry today." We stood for a moment and watched the tide building below us. The Severn Bore is famous all over the world. The river is a mile wide at this point so there's plenty of room for the water to pass upstream, but a little further on, it becomes much narrower. On a high spring tide, with nowhere to go, the great surge of water builds into a large wave that carries on as far as Gloucester. My grandmother had often taken me to Minsterworth to watch the Bore pass, warning me to keep well away from the river bank as the Bore rushed by. She would point out the strange things that would be swept past us. Whole trees, garden tables, garden fences would sail past. I remembered seeing a fridge and a table and chairs on one occasion. Although it was a spectacular sight, I was always happy to watch it from a distance, safe from its destructive power.

Another tug on the leash told me that Dotty wanted to be on the move again and I noticed how her pace had quickened by the time we had reached the end of the track. As we crossed the top on the outer lock gate, she was travelling at a gallop until I pulled her up sharp when we drew level with the wall of the Yacht Club's compound.

"Perhaps the tide's spooking her," said Bob.

I thought it unlikely, as she loved to be near water and besides, instead of running away from it, she appeared to want to go towards it. A patch of land between the side of the Old Shipyard House and the river, was known as 'The Marsh' and we had always been told to stay away from it. Although it was not real marshland, dense reeds concealed a bank of soft, thick mud beneath. Local children would tell stories of people being sucked into it and never seen again. Although I did not believe any of them, I still preferred to keep my distance. However, Dotty's destination seemed to be in that direction, so we followed her to where the first reeds stuck up like an unruly fringe from the land. At that point, the undergrowth softened the roar of the river and from somewhere amongst the reeds, we heard a faint cry: Someone was calling for help. Dotty had stopped, her ears pricked as she listened for the sound again. When it came, her reaction told us all we needed to know, because she became that venomous snake once more, flattening her ears and hissing viciously.

"Blender!" said Bob in amazement. "What's she doing here?"

As if in answer to his question, another voice cried out, "We're stuck in the reeds. We tried to push ourselves off, but lost the oars."

This was followed by a loud wail from Blender, who cried out, "We're all going to die!"

"Drama queen," muttered Bob, then shouted back, "Hold on while we go and find help."

"Wait here," he said to me, "while I run and get Billy O."

I was glad when he returned with Grandma and Billy O, as by now, the water was creeping up the slipway behind me and I started to feel that I would be cut off if the harbour flooded.

"I think she's with Phil Renney and Dave Higgins," said Bob. "I recognised Phil's voice."

"Birds of a feather flock together," said Grandma. There was no time to ask what she meant, because Billy O shouted out, "All hands to the pump," and opened the Safety Boat hut.

'Here we go again," said Grandma, looking towards the sky and shaking her head.

"Bring the cat," said Billy O.

"Of nine tails?" questioned Grandma, "That's what I'd like to bring to that madam!"

Dotty chirped with excitement as she was lifted aboard the safety boat. As we made ready to launch, Billy O disappeared into the hut again. Grandma took the opportunity to call 999 and request assistance, in case it was needed.

"He'd better hurry up," said Grandma, "I reckon we've got less than twenty minutes, then… whoosh!"

"What's 'whoosh'?" I asked.

"Whoosh is what will happen to madam and her friends when this tide reaches its peak. They will either be tipped into the reeds or they'll be swept free of the weeds and carried up onto the rocks above them. On this tide, the boat will surely be smashed to smithereens … and them with it!"

I gasped, because although I did not like Blender, I did not like to think of her becoming a 'smithereen', whatever that was.

"Got it," said Billy O as he emerged from the shed waving a spool of fishing line.

So much water now covered the slipway that launching the safety boat was easy. However, even with its powerful engine, it was difficult to stem the tide and I was pleased that we did not have to venture far from the slipway, before we could see the stern of the little blue tender poking out of the reeds.

"We can't get too close," said Billy O, 'or we'll get stuck too."

He turned to my grandmother and said, "Melissa, we need your cat's help."

He explained that he would attach one end of the fishing line to SMALL DOG and the other to a mooring line. Dotty would swim out to the stranded tender, taking the fishing line with her. Phil Renney would then be able to haul in the fishing line and draw the heavier rope after it. Once that was attached, we would be able to tow them back to safety.

Grandma looked from her cat to the blue boat and back again and said quietly,

"We have no choice."

"There's one problem," said Bob. "Dotty hates Blender and won't go any where near her."

I remembered the cat's reaction when she had heard Blender's voice through the reeds and knew that what he was saying was true. Suddenly, I had an idea and called out to the tender,

"Have you got any food on board?"

"Nothing much," shouted Phil Renney, "There's only a half-eaten ham sandwich."

I smiled and called back,

"Wave it over the stern of the boat when we tell you."

Billy O attached one end of the fine line to Dotty's lifejacket and the other to a strong mooring line, explaining that the weight of the heavy rope would be too much for an animal as small as Dotty to carry through the strong current.

"Ready?' asked Billy O.

Giving Dotty one last hug, Grandma nodded, "Ready."

"Ready," I shouted in the direction of the stranded boat and watched as a hand appeared over the stern and waved a ham sandwich in our direction.

Dotty did not need any more encouragement than a ham sandwich, even a half-eaten one. With a great splash, she launched herself into the water and with a few firm strokes of her strong legs, reached the boat and was lifted aboard. We watched as the fishing line was hauled in, the rope snaking through the water behind it. When it had been securely tied to the stern, Billy O thrust the motor of the safety boat into reverse and slowly, very slowly, the blue boat emerged from the reeds. We reached the top of the slipway with ease, as the water was now at its highest point. After quickly clambering out, we hauled on the line to bring the little, blue tender safely ashore.

The blare of sirens along the path to the Old Shipyard House, announced the arrival of an ambulance and a police car, while down the river we could see a Severn Area Rescue Association boat heading in our direction.

They all arrived as we were about to help Blender, Phil, Dave and, of course Dotty onto dry land, but were stopped by a sudden cry from behind.

"Wait!" a familiar voice called out. "Just one picture, if you please?"

I turned to see Mr Williamson, the reporter from the *Clarion* raising his camera and taking an 'action photograph of the daring rescue', as the caption read in that afternoon's edition of the newspaper. It was followed by an account of how three teenagers had taken a small boat out onto the River Severn and would have been swept away, if it had not been for the prompt actions of Captain William O'Donnell, Mrs Melissa Gates, Megan Waterfield, Robert Robertson and of course that old friend of the *Clarion*, Dotty the Salty Sea Cat. Another picture showed the rescuers posed in front of the little blue tender. On its prow sat Dotty and the caption underneath said that she had carried out the rescue, almost 'single-pawed', although she could not have done so without the ingenuity of Captain O'Donnell and the bravery of his crew.

Apparently, when Blender had been banned from the Old Harbour, she had visited the local park, where she had met Phil and Dave.

"Mischief finds mischief," said Grandma, nodding her head sadly.

All three of them felt angry about the way people had treated them and planned a small revenge. Early that morning, they had taken the tender from the pontoon and decided to sail it to Gloucester, where they would abandon it and take the bus home. Not one of them had any experience of sailing, other than on the lake in the park, and not one of them had thought to look at the tide table.

"It's a good job they thought to take some ham sandwiches," chuckled Billy O.

As Blender got into the police car, she turned to Grandma and said,

"I'm sorry for what I did to your cat. She saved my life."

I don't think that my grandmother had expected an apology and for once, spoke simply.

"That's all right," she said. "Just make sure you live that life well, from now on."

"What will happen to her?" I asked, as the police car drove away.

"Oh, a telling off, I daresay," said Grandma. "Let's hope she's learnt her lesson, this time."

Later that day, we actually managed to unload everything from the Fiona and, with the Land Rover 'loaded to the scuppers', we trundled back to *Graymalkin Cottage.* As we turned into the lane, Grandma asked,

"Was that enough 'Derring Do' for you?"

"I think that would be enough for anyone," I laughed.

That evening, we sat at the kitchen table and Grandma cut out several copies of the article from the pile of newspapers in front of us, while I completed my log.

Hey ho," sighed Grandma, "I suppose this will mean more medals."

The photograph of my grandfather that hung in the Fiona's cabin during the sailing season, now stood on the Welsh dresser in the kitchen. The plaque that bore his name, was newly polished, so that the words, 'Captain Andrew Gates' stood out clearly and boldly. Its gold frame was festooned with the medals we had been awarded earlier that year. As I climbed the stairs to bed, I heard my grandmother's voice from the kitchen and wondered for a moment who she could be talking to, until I heard her say,

"Well, Andrew, wasn't that the cat's pyjamas?"

When Ma arrived the next day, I was so full of the stories of my stay at *Graymalkin Cottage*, that she hardly had chance to tell us about her holiday.

Although I was glad to see her, I was sad that half-term was over and there would be no more visits to the Old Harbour until the spring.

Chapter 10

At the end of the following summer, Grandma received a letter. Although it was addressed to her, an accompanying note said that it should be shared with, Bob, Billy O and me. It read,

'Dear Mrs Gates,

At the invitation of Mr Dunbarry, I have spent the summer in Scotland. He wanted me to be present at the unveiling of the museum's latest exhibit. The picture on the enclosed postcard will tell you what that exhibit is, although I'm sure you have already guessed. They have done such a fine job on her, that I can't believe that she was ever the Rat Boat.

I would like to thank you all for helping me to do what my great-uncle asked of me. I don't think I've let him down and like to think how proud he would be if he could see the 'Red Skye' as she is now.

As for me, I am learning to sail and in two years time, I will buy my own boat. I would like to name her the 'Fiona II', if that is all right with you.

Ryan.'

The postcard that accompanied the letter had a picture on the front. It showed a ring netter in the twilight. It was painted red and had a familiar high prow with its hawse hole eye picked out in gold. Beneath it was written the boat's name and across the bottom of the photograph ran the caption, 'The *Red Skye* at Sunset'.

Glossary

Fer ye landlubbers!

Many of you young 'uns have asked what some of the nautical terms used in the stories mean.

This will help you to understand:

Bow: or prow is the front of the boat

Stern: the back of the boat

Port: the left side, when you are facing the bow

Starboard: the right side

Fore: at the front

Aft: at, near, or towards the stern of the boat

Cockpit: the area where the captain steers the boat from

Companion way: the entrance to the cabins from the cockpit

Washboard: a wooden hatch that covers the companion way

Cabin: a room inside a boat. The *Fiona* has two cabins: the saloon and the fore cabin

Berth: can mean where you sleep on the boat or where the boat is kept

Jib: a triangular sail at the front or fore of the boat

Moor: to tie the boat to something, so that it does not float away

Wheelhouse: a covered cabin on the deck of larger boats or ships, from where the captain controls the boat

Hold: an area below decks where cargo can be stored

Bilge: the lowest part of the boat where any water that has seeped in, collects

Hull: the boat's outer body. The *Fiona*'s is painted blue

Silt: fine sand

Lifebelt: a large ring that is made from a material that floats

Bulwark: the part of the boat's side that is above the deck, making a wall

Gunwale: the top edge of the side of the boat

Scuppers: holes in the bulwark that carry water from the deck

Lock: a chamber with gates at either end. They can be opened or closed to raise or lower the water level

Hawse hole: an eye-shaped hole in the prow of a boat through which mooring lines or cables can pass

About the 'Old Harbour'

The Old Harbour is based on Lydney Harbour in Gloucestershire. I sometimes change little things about it to make the story work, but I try to give as true a picture of this beautiful place, as possible. It was a very important harbour from Roman times until the twentieth century and is now protected as a Scheduled Ancient Monument.

The harbour has several parts:

The Outer Basin is the area closest to the River Severn and is entered through large lock gates.

The Inner or Lower Basin is entered from the Outer Basin by another lock. It is here that most of the boats are moored.

The Swing Bridge is found at the end of the Inner Basin, and marks the beginning of the canal.

The Lydney Canal is one mile long, but it is not possible to use the whole length because of weed cover. The canal is fed by the River Lyd.

Lydney Yacht Club is based in the Old Shipyard House, right on the edge of the River Severn.

Made in the USA
Columbia, SC
05 May 2017